THE MOON SPEAKS CREE

A Winter Adventure

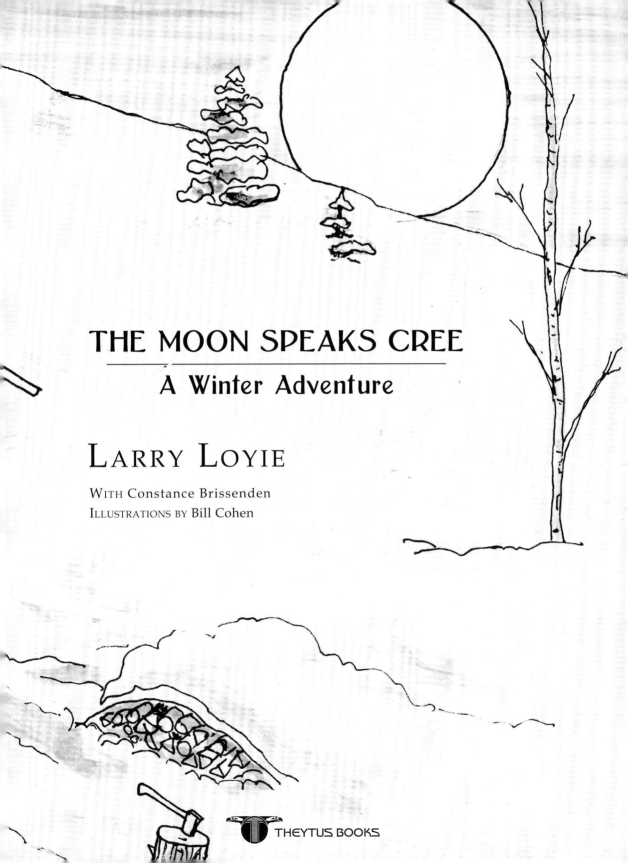

THE MOON SPEAKS CREE

A Winter Adventure

LARRY LOYIE

WITH Constance Brissenden
ILLUSTRATIONS BY Bill Cohen

THEYTUS BOOKS

Library and Archives Canada Cataloguing in Publication

Loyie, Larry, 1933-, author
The moon speaks Cree : a winter adventure / Larry Loyie with Constance
Brissenden ; illustrations by Bill Cohen.

ISBN 978-1-926886-18-3 (pbk.)

I. Brissenden, Constance, 1947-, author II. Cohen, Bill, 1963-, illustrator
III. Title.

PS8573.O979M66 2013   jC813'.6   C2012-903022-8

Printed in Canada

THEYTUS BOOKS
Publishing Indigenous Voices

Published by Theytus Books
www.theytus.com

Thank you Jordan Wheeler for your excellent editing.

 Canadian   Patrimoine
Heritage   canadien

 Canada Council   Conseil des Arts
for the Arts   du Canada

 BRITISH COLUMBIA
ARTS COUNCIL
Supported by the Province of British Columbia

We acknowledge the financial support of The Government of Canada
through the Department of Canadian heritage for our publishing
activities. We acknowledge the support of the Canada Council for
the Arts, which last year invested $154 million to bring the arts to
Canadians throughout the country. *Nous remercions le Conseil des arts du
Canada de son soutien. L'an dernier, le Conseil a investi 154 millions de dollars
pour mettre de l'art dans la vie des Canadiennes et des Canadiens de tout le pays.*
We acknowledge the support of the Province of British Columbia
through the British Columbia Arts Council

The year is 1940, the season is winter, a time of adventure and learning for Aboriginal children. Larry Loyie, known as Lawrence, is learning the traditional way of life he loves to this day.

Table of Contents

Chapter 1
The Old Trunk

"Winter will be here soon," Lawrence said aloud, a small voice in the big forest. He walked alone, studying the trees that surrounded him. A few yellow leaves still clung to the poplars.

He was young but he could already read the seasons by the signs of nature. "If you look hard enough, you will see changes every day," his grandfather, Mosoom Albert, had taught him.

Lawrence bent over to pick up a bright red leaf, his grandmother's favorite colour. 'This dropped here just for Kokom Bella,' he decided. He smiled as he tucked it in his shirt pocket.

Nearing home, he saw one snowflake fall, then another. Soon the air was filled with big fluffy flakes.

Watching in silence, he heard the *ching, ching, ching* of Papa's axe as it hit a hard tamarack log and the sound of Robert, his older brother, sawing logs for the wood stove. His two sisters, Margaret and Elizabeth, were nowhere in sight.

He hurried into the log house to tell them the news. "I saw the first snowflake!" He boasted. The two girls pushed past him and rushed out to see for themselves. Lawrence's dog Buster bounded over to see what the excitement was all about.

"Let's go sliding on Rabbit Hill," little sister Margaret said as she jumped up and down. "We'll need a lot more snow," Lawrence teased her. Being older he didn't want to admit he was thinking the same thing.

Big sister Elizabeth frowned. "We have nothing to slide on," she said, then shivered. "It's cold out here. Come inside and play with us."

Lawrence shook his head. The last time he played with his sisters he was a clothesline pole, holding the ends of a piece of string for them to hang their doll clothes. 'I'm not doing that again,' he thought.

He followed the girls back into the house. The heat from the wood stove made the living room warm and cozy.

Mama sat on a bear rug sewing a pair of winter moccasins for Papa. She watched as Lawrence walked over. "I thought you were playing with your sisters," she said, nodding toward the girls.

"It's no fun being Elizabeth's clothesline pole. I'd rather help you."

Mama laughed. "Good. I can use your help. Let's get out the winter coats." She put her sewing away in a basket. I'll finish Papa's moccasins tomorrow. He's going to his trapline soon. He'll need a second pair."

With Lawrence's help, Mama hauled a battered trunk to the centre of the room. The girls jumped up to watch. Their mother flipped the dull brass latch and lifted the worn brown lid. The lid broke off and fell to the floor with a thud.

"This old trunk has finally fallen apart." Mama gazed at it thoughtfully. "This steamer trunk belonged to your grandfather Daniel. He died in the flu epidemic of 1918. Many of our people died at that time," she said sadly.

Lawrence tried to imagine Papa's father who had died long ago. "I wish I could have met him," he said to Mama. She nodded. "I wish that too," she replied.

Mama got back to work. She pulled out a blue winter coat and handed it to Margaret. "This was Elizabeth's. Now it's yours." Margaret slipped it on and twirled around. Even though she was two years younger than Lawrence, she was almost as tall as he was. The coat fit her just right.

Next was a green wool jacket for Elizabeth. "Your cousin in town gave you this," Mama said.

Big sister tried it on and went to the mirror. She buttoned it up and smiled. "It's pretty," she said proudly.

"Now it's your turn, Lawrence." Mama helped him squeeze into his last-year coat. The sleeves were short and his wrists stuck out.

Lawrence made a face.

"That won't do," Mama said. "You have grown so much. You'll have to wear Robert's old jacket. It will be big but I'll fix it for you." She took it out.

Lawrence was surprised at how small Robert's jacket looked. His brother was almost as tall as Papa now and wore his father's old work coat. He went to school in town and did odd jobs when he wasn't helping at home.

'He never plays with me anymore,' Lawrence thought as he looked at the jacket. He loved his sisters but he missed his brother's company.

The trunk was finally empty. Together Mama and Lawrence carried it outside and set it under the eaves of the house. "You can play with this if you want. I'll get another one soon," Mama said. She went inside, snowflakes dotting her short dark hair.

Lawrence studied her gift. What could he do with Mosoom Daniel's trunk? Suddenly, he had an idea. With the lid off, it was big enough to sit in.

"Tansi!"

Lawrence jumped in surprise. Kokom Bella stood beside him with her dog Whiskers. She had come down quietly from her home nearby to visit them.

Lawrence jumped in surprise.
Kokom Bella stood beside
him.

"Tansi, Kokom," Lawrence greeted her. "This is for you." He handed her the red leaf from his pocket.

"You remembered that red is my favorite colour," Kokom said. "You make me very happy." She kissed him on the forehead.

Kokom wore her ski pants under her long skirt.

"You look like you're ready for winter," Lawrence observed.

"We're leaving for our trapline soon," Kokom grinned happily, "Uncle Moses, Dave Auger and me. Everything is ready."

"What's it like on your trapline?" Lawrence asked. He knew it was a day's walk.

"Our cabin is snug and safe. The forest is like a food store. When we want something special to eat, we go hunting for it."

Kokom spied the old trunk. "I'm sorry to see that go. It was the only thing around here that was older than me," she chuckled.

"Mama gave it to me. I don't know what to do with it."

"If I know you, you'll think of something," Kokom replied.

They went into the house together. The delicious smell of rabbit stew cooking on the wood stove welcomed them.

Chapter 2
Toboggan Day

Lawrence and Buster walked to a clearing in the forest where the snow was deep. With a tin plate, the boy dug down to the older snow underneath. It shone like crystals. A noisy Blue Jay landed on a poplar branch nearby. Buster watched and waited patiently.

"Good boy," Lawrence said and patted him on his rusty-coloured head. "I'll be finished soon." He opened up a flour sack and started to fill it with heavy packed snow for his mother's washing. When it melted later, the heavy snow from the bottom would make more water than the light snow from the top. After the sack was full, Lawrence dragged it back to the house.

His mother dumped the contents into her washtub. "Go out and help Papa now," she said. "He's getting the toboggan ready to leave for his trapline."

Papa came around the corner of the shed pulling his long wooden toboggan. At the sight of him, the four dogs in the yard began to bark.

Buster howled and ran in circles. Sport, the biggest of Papa's dogs, added loud woof woofs. Friendly Brownie yipped and tugged at his rope. Sad-faced Buckskin's deep barks added to the din.

Margaret ran up to Lawrence. "Why are the dogs acting crazy?" She asked breathlessly. She stood as far back from them as possible.

"They know I'm leaving soon," Papa observed. "It's hard work pulling a toboggan but they enjoy it."

The dogs trembled with excitement as they watched Papa. First he checked the leather harnesses to make sure they were soft and comfortable. He had rubbed them with goose grease last fall to keep them from cracking.

As Papa worked, he told Lawrence, "Make sure you always treat your dogs well. They are working animals. If something happens to one of them on the trail, you'll have to help the others do the pulling."

While Lawrence watched, his father harnessed the dogs. Sport was first. He quivered and shook. "Sport will pull at the back. He's the strongest," Papa told him.

Big Buckskin was next. He was clumsy but he pulled his heart out when it was time to work. Smaller Brownie was placed second from the front. He was orange in colour. Lawrence always wondered why he was called Brownie until his father explained, "Brownie was an easy name for you children to remember."

As the lead dog, Buster knew the commands of right and left.

First in line was Buster. As the lead dog, Buster knew the commands of right and left. Buster had bad habits as well as good ones. If he had to work, he would sneak away and hide in the forest. Papa added a small chain when he hitched Buster to his harness.

"He can't wiggle out of the harness and run away now," Lawrence told Margaret.

Howling, barking, woofing and yipping, the dogs were eager to go.

"I leave tomorrow," Papa said. "Today I have to haul winter wood for the house. I'll take the dogs for a trial run to pick it up. Want to come for a ride?"

"Yes, yes," Margaret shrieked.

Lawrence smiled and helped her settle on the toboggan, then jumped on behind her. His hands gripped the rope along the side.

"Mush!" Papa called. With a jerk, the dogs took off, barking loudly.

"Hold on," Lawrence yelled to Margaret as they bumped along. The dogs began to work well together. The toboggan picked up speed. Lawrence laughed with excitement.

Sometimes Papa ran behind to give the dogs a break. At other times, he stood on the back to slow the toboggan down. They soon topped a hill, drawing up near the pile of birch logs Papa had cut the summer before.

"Whoa!" Papa shouted. The team shuddered to a halt. "Good dogs.

You did well for the first run of the season," he praised them. As Lawrence and Margaret got off, the dogs flopped down on the trail. They panted hard, their tongues hanging out, their breath making white puffs in the air.

"Hold this rope Lawrence while I shift the logs." As the children watched, Papa chose three logs from the pile and lifted them on the long toboggan. He put two more on top of them and one more on top of the two. With Lawrence's help, he tied them securely to the toboggan. "This way they can't roll," Papa said.

'Robert will have to saw a lot of logs,' Lawrence thought. For the first time he realized that being almost grown-up meant his older brother had to work hard.

Soon Papa was ready to head home. Lawrence and his sister walked behind as the dogs scrambled to pull the heavy load. Now and then, their father stopped to rest the animals. "The dogs are tired," Lawrence said. "Will they make it all the way home?"

"They want to keep going," Papa reassured him. "They love to run in the forest. After this heavy load, pulling my supplies will be much easier."

Back in the yard, Margaret watched Lawrence give each dog a share of wild meat. The animals ate eagerly and then lay down to rest after a hard-working day.

Snow began to fall. "I can catch a snowflake with my tongue," Lawrence challenged Margaret.

"So can I," she shot back. "You're not the only one." Lawrence ran in circles, stabbing the air with his tongue. Margaret darted back and forth. Try as they might, neither one caught a snowflake. Lawrence didn't mind. 'I have all winter,' he told himself thankfully. Winter was his favorite season.

The sun was setting and they felt cold for the first time. "Let's go in," he said to Margaret.

Chapter 3
Saying Goodbye

The next morning, Papa and Robert were up early packing the toboggan and harnessing the dogs. Lawrence slipped out of bed when he heard them move about. He dressed quickly and went outside. Mama had shifted the buttons on Robert's old winter jacket and he didn't feel the cold at all.

Papa brought out a wooden apple box. "Can I help you?" Lawrence asked shyly. He was four years younger than Robert but he wanted to be useful. Papa agreed, and Lawrence helped him pack his food supplies in the box, including flour, sugar, salt, baking powder, lard, tea, jam and peanut butter.

"This is all I need for a month in the bush," Papa said. "These supplies and wild meat will keep me fed."

"What will the dogs eat?" Lawrence asked.

"The dogs will eat well. They like wild meat too. Nothing is ever wasted."

"Will you come home for Christmas?" Lawrence wanted to know.

Papa grinned. "I wouldn't miss our Christmas dinner for anything. I'll be back after I make some money to keep our family going this winter."

He tied his warm parka on top of his supplies. "While I'm away, bring in wood and snow for your mother when she needs them," he instructed Lawrence.

He turned to Robert. "Keep your mother stocked with wood," he ordered. Robert nodded. As usual, he didn't say much.

Mama came out of the house carrying a big bannock wrapped in a clean cloth. It would feed Papa for many days. The aroma of the fresh baking was tempting.

Elizabeth and Margaret came outside to say goodbye.

"I'll miss you, Buster." Lawrence gave Buster a hug.

"I'll miss you, Sport," Margaret said. Sport was her favorite dog.

Standing together, the family watched as Papa set out. The dogs barked and strained to pull the toboggan.

"Papa knows how to do everything," Lawrence said as his father disappeared down Forestry Road.

"He began young just like you," Mama said. "You already know a lot. You will do well if you always watch and listen."

The dogs barked and strained to pull the toboggan.

Chapter 4
The Whitford Sled

Robert's sled was the most beautiful in the world. Lawrence studied it closely. He admired the steel on the wooden runners that made it slide smooth and fast on the snow. Robert called it his Whitford sled because it was homemade by the Whitford brothers of nearby Canyon Creek. To buy it, he had worked hard in town doing odd jobs. He was the only teenager in the town of Slave Lake to own one.

"I'll have a sled like this one day," Lawrence boldly told his sisters.

The three children stared at the sled, afraid to touch it. It was special to Robert and they knew it.

Their older brother was nowhere to be seen. Lawrence hoped he was in town. He looked around to make sure.

The sled begged him to try it out. "It won't hurt if I just sit on it," he said.

Elizabeth gasped. "Robert will be angry if he catches you."

"Don't do it," Margaret moaned.

Lawrence moved close to the sled as if he didn't hear them. He sat down on it.

"Get off Robert's sled," Elizabeth warned him.

Lawrence picked up the rope at the front as if he were sliding down Rabbit Hill.

"Yahoo!" He yelled. One hand in the air, he pretended to ride the sled like a wild bronco.

"Get off!" Robert appeared from nowhere, a scowl on his face. "You're not allowed on it!" Lawrence scrambled off as fast as he could. His sisters scurried out of the way. Robert grabbed the rope and pulled his sled away.

Robert grabbed the rope and pulled his sled away.

"Let us have one ride," Lawrence called bravely after him.

"It's mine," Robert said over his shoulder. "Don't touch it again."

They went in the house to tell Mama. She stood back, her hands on her hips. "Your brother uses his sled for his chores and he does odd jobs in town. He also goes to school. If you broke it, it would be hard for him to get his work done. Understand?"

Heads hung low, Lawrence and his sisters went back outside.

"We can't go sliding," Margaret said with tears in her eyes.

"Yes, we can," Lawrence said. "We'll make do with what we have. That's what Kokom always says."

While the girls waited, Lawrence walked into Papa's shed and looked around. He picked up a piece of torn cardboard, left the shed and called to his sisters. "Follow me!"

"What's he got?" Margaret asked Elizabeth.

"It doesn't look like much," said Elizabeth doubtfully.

Lawrence marched over to the sliding hill, his sisters close behind. They could see the smoke from the chimneys in the town below.

Lawrence dropped the cardboard on the snow and sat on it. It was small and he could barely grab the edges. "Give me a push," he advised Elizabeth.

With Elizabeth pushing, he kicked his moccasins against the snow. He started to move forward slowly.

Margaret clapped her hands. "You're sliding!"

Elizabeth stepped away as Lawrence picked up speed.

"Whoa!" With a shout, Lawrence slipped off the cardboard, rolled over and came to a halt. Elizabeth and Margaret laughed and watched him get back on the cardboard. This time he didn't move an inch. He stood up and shrugged his shoulders. "Want to try it?" He asked his sisters.

"Not me," Elizabeth said. Margaret shook her head.

They trudged back to the house. Leaning against the logs, the old trunk caught Lawrence's eye. He stopped so suddenly his sisters bumped into him. "What's up?" Elizabeth asked.

Lawrence didn't answer. Instead, he brushed the snow off the trunk. He dug in his mind for ideas.

Finally he said, "We can use this." He removed the lid and motioned to his sisters to step in and sit down. Once they were settled at the front, he climbed in behind them. They all fit nicely.

Elizabeth climbed out. "How can we make it go?" She said.

Lawrence jumped out. "Let's push it and see if it slides." They tried pushing Margaret in the trunk, but the snow stuck on the four brass corners. The trunk wouldn't move at all.

"It's getting dark. We have to go in," Lawrence said reluctantly. With his sisters' help, he pulled the trunk back under the eaves of their house.

"Look! A diamond!" Elizabeth pointed at a bright star that sparkled above them.

Lawrence gazed at the sky. A full moon had appeared, so close he felt he could almost touch it. The moon seemed to speak to him. "Kayas," it said. "It's been a long time."

As they headed in for supper, the words of Mosoom Albert came back to him. "You know how to think out problems. I like that about you."

Thinking it out, Lawrence got the glimmer of an idea.

Chapter 5
The Amazing Slider

The moon cast bright shadows over the land. Lawrence imagined Papa sitting comfortably in his cabin in the forest. The dogs would be asleep in their huts nearby.

"Can I go sliding?" He asked Mama. She was darning socks by lamplight. Elizabeth had washed the dishes while Margaret dried and put them away.

"You may, Lawrence, and your sisters can go with you." She looked out the window at the full moon shining on the new snow. "It's bright as daylight out there."

As he put on his winter jacket, Lawrence shared his secret. "I have an idea about our slider," he told his sisters. "Wait and see." He slipped out the front door. Curious, they watched him go.

Inside the shed, Lawrence hauled down a scoop shovel from its nail on the wall. He picked up a flattened piece of tin from an old fifty-pound bulk peanut butter container and carried the shovel and the tin outside.

"Let's go," he called to his sisters. As they hurried out to join him, Lawrence handed Elizabeth the scoop shovel and gave Margaret the tin. With Lawrence dragging the trunk, they made their way to the sliding hill.

"I want to lift the four corners off the snow," Lawrence explained. He tucked the scoop shovel under the front of the trunk. Next he set the back of the trunk on the tin and tied it with a rope. He surveyed his invention.

"It's ready now," he announced, more confidently than he felt.

Margaret stepped in and sat down. Elizabeth snuggled in next.

They screamed with laughter as they flew down the hill.

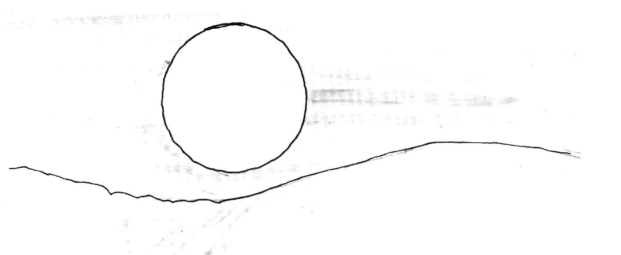

When they were settled,
Lawrence ran behind pushing hard.

"Hold on! Here we go!" He yelled. As the trunk began to move on its own, he jumped in.

The shovel slid smoothly. Lawrence did not even need to steer. "It works! My slider works!" He shouted. They whizzed over the snow. Eyes wide, Elizabeth held Margaret tightly. They screamed with laughter as they flew down the hill.

At the bottom, they slowed to a stop. Lawrence raised his arms in victory. "I did it! My slider really works!"

Elizabeth jumped out. "Let's do it again!" Her excited voice echoed in the starry night. Margaret bobbed her head up and down in agreement. She had laughed so hard she couldn't speak.

Pushing and shoving, they hauled the trunk, the shovel and the tin back up the hill. A figure waited for them at the top. It was Robert standing beside his sled.

"We have the fastest slider in the whole world," Lawrence called out to him.

"Can I try it?" Robert asked.

Lawrence could hardly believe what he heard. Robert wanted to try his slider. 'You're too big,' he thought. He didn't dare say it out loud. "Try it," he said instead. "It's fun."

Robert climbed into the trunk and tried to sit down, but his long legs would not fold up enough to fit. He knelt down, but he was still too big. He climbed out of the trunk. "I guess I don't fit," he admitted. He pointed to his sled. "I'm gonna try mine. You can take it for a ride after I finish."

"Do you mean it?" Lawrence asked. He couldn't remember the last time Robert played with him. Was he teasing? Lawrence wanted to believe Robert but he didn't trust him. His older brother was like a stranger.

"I mean it," said Robert gruffly. "Look, I'll show you how it's done. I don't want you to wreck it." He pushed the sled easily from behind, then threw himself face down on it. His feet hung out the back as a guide.

As Lawrence and his sisters watched with awe, Robert swooped down the hill. At the bottom he stood up easily and slapped the snow off his pants.

After he climbed back up, it was Lawrence's turn. His heart beat fast as he pushed the sled forward. He had never ridden a real one before. 'I can do it,' he promised himself. 'If Robert can do it, so can I.' He gritted his teeth and jumped on.

The steel runners flew along the snow. Lawrence sped down the hill, faster than ever in his life. "I can slide forever," he hollered as the hill whooshed by him. Without warning, the sled began to sway from side to side. In an instant, it flipped against a rut, tossing him high into the air. He landed on a snow bank.

As he lay on the snow, tears came to his eyes. He held them back. 'If Robert sees me cry he'll never let me try again,' he thought. Then he shivered. 'Did I wreck Robert's sled?' He asked himself fearfully. He sat up slowly and looked down the hill. The sled lay in one piece at the bottom.

He heard noises. "Are you alright?" His sisters shouted from above.

Robert was bent over, clutching his sides. "You make a good airplane," he howled with laughter. "Next time, remember to hang on. Use your feet to steer. Drag your right foot to go right and your left to go left."

Lawrence was angry. How was he supposed to know to hang on or use his feet to steer? He'd never ridden a real sled before. Then he realized. Robert had said, "Next time."

'I'll show him I can do it,' Lawrence vowed. He stood up and began to pull his brother's sled up the hill for another try.

Chapter 6
A Visit From Jack Frost

Christmas was only a week away. When they could, the children watched at the front window for Papa's return.

Overnight, Jack Frost had visited and completely covered the window panes with his sparkly silver etchings. Lawrence pressed his thumb against the frost to make a peephole. Peering out, he saw that nothing moved in the snow-covered forest. He sighed in disappointment and stepped back.

"Look at this," Lawrence said to his sisters. "Jack Frost left us something last night." The girls looked up from their dolls, got to their feet and came over.

"Who is Jack Frost?" Asked Margaret.

"He's a little person who visits in winter," Elizabeth told her. "Nobody sees him but he leaves his frosty pictures behind."

Lawrence pointed at the window. "Here's a bull moose with the biggest antlers I've ever seen. And here's Papa's cabin." The girls looked closely. Sure enough, they saw the shape of Papa's cabin.

Elizabeth got a dreamy look on her face. "Here's my new Christmas dress from the mail order catalogue," she said, pointing to a spot on the pane. Lawrence couldn't see it, but he nodded anyway.

Standing on her tiptoes, Margaret peered at the window. "I can see Christmas candies. I wish I could have one now," she said loudly for Mama's benefit. Mama did not turn her head, only smiled to herself. The candies were tucked away in a secret place until Christmas Day.

"Where do you see the candies?" Lawrence asked.

Margaret showed him the swirls in the frost. "They're twirly ribbon candies. Red and white and green."

"You can't see colours in frost," Lawrence said.

"Yes, I can," Margaret replied, sure of herself. "I can dream too, you know."

In the late afternoon they were surprised to hear the dogs barking and Papa's voice calling. He was smiling when they hurried out to greet him.

"We'll have a good Christmas this year," he told his family. "I did well on my trapline."

With Papa safely back, the children knew that Christmas could really begin.

"Look at this," Lawrence said to his sisters. "Jack Frost left us something last night."

Chapter 7
Christmas Bells and Snowshoes

Lawrence and Robert went with Papa to cut a spruce tree for the house. "You can choose the Christmas tree," Papa told Lawrence. "We'll load it on Robert's sled." Lawrence searched carefully. He chose one that was not too big and not too small.

Back at home, he helped Margaret and Elizabeth decorate it with red crepe paper streamers, green and red paper bells and silver tinsel. Then Mama went to the shed and came back with her special box of shiny ornaments. She hung them with care. They all stood back to admire their work.

"Our tree is beautiful," said Elizabeth. Lawrence added a red bell to fill in a hole.

"Now it's perfect," Mama said. Lawrence thought so too.

Margaret searched for the best place to hang her stocking. "I don't want Santa to miss it." She moved it from one branch to another on the tree. Finally she chose one that was easy for Santa to spot.

The children tried to stay awake on Christmas Eve to see Santa. Try as they might, they all fell asleep.

On Christmas morning, they found ribbon candies and a juicy Japanese orange inside their stockings.

Santa brought Margaret a doll with eyes that closed when she lay it down. Elizabeth wore her new blue and white hair barrettes to match her catalogue dress. Robert got a red checkered shirt and warm brown mitts. Lawrence was proud of his red toy tractor with its shiny paint.

No one wanted to eat breakfast but Mama insisted. "Christmas dinner will be a while," she said.

In the early afternoon, Papa told Lawrence, "Keep watch at the window for guests." Kokom Bella, her son Moses and her friend Dave were the first to arrive. Kokom's dog Whiskers stayed outside.

Soon after, a lone figure came up the hill. "It's Mosoom Albert," Lawrence announced. He rushed outside. His soft-spoken grandfather had slipped his snowshoes off and set them against the house. "Tansi, Mosoom," Lawrence greeted him.

"Kayas, Grandson," Mosoom Albert smiled his gentle smile. "You look healthy. I'm glad to see that." He noticed Lawrence admiring his snowshoes. "I made them long and narrow so I could take longer strides when I walk in deep snow. When you're older, we'll go snowshoeing together," he promised Lawrence. "I'll make a special pair just your size."

"When you're older, we'll go snowshoeing together," Mosoom promised Lawrence.

"We have a giant turkey, big enough for everybody," Lawrence smiled in reply. "We have your favorite cooked raspberries too."

They went inside and joined the party at the table. Mama piled every plate high with delicious foods and poured steaming tea into cups. Mosoom cooled his tea in a saucer, smacking his lips. "Wihkasin. Tasty! Your cooking must be good, Marie. No one has time to talk," he joked.

Kokom winked at Lawrence. "Wait until he tastes your Mama's plum pudding with cream. He'll be speechless too."

Whiskers ate with the other dogs in the yard. Even they had a Christmas treat. Buster and his companions enjoyed chewing on their special meal of leftover moose bones, growling at any dog coming near their food.

Chapter 8
Don't Tease Sport

Lawrence carried an armful of wood into the house and then went out for more. Mama was hanging clothes to dry in the fresh winter air. In the yard, Robert fed the dogs. Lawrence watched him dangle a piece of meat above Buster's head. Buster lunged but missed it.

"Give Buster his food," Lawrence shouted at his older brother.

Laughing, Robert dropped the meat. Buster grabbed it hungrily.

Lawrence ran to tell Mama but she had already seen for herself. Frowning, she warned Robert, "Don't tease the dogs. One of them will hurt you for being so mean."

"I won't tease them," Robert replied. He fed Buckskin and Brownie next.

Sport was last. He wagged his tail playfully. Holding the meat high, Robert danced it over Sport's head. The big dog snapped at the food but missed. "Try again," Robert taunted him.

This time Mama's voice was sharp and strict. "Stop it! The dogs don't like it. I won't tell you again."

Sport jumped, his jaws open. In an instant, he sank his teeth deep into Robert's face. Just as swiftly the big dog let go, snatched his meat and ate it quickly. He growled a warning.

Robert screamed. Clutching his face, he staggered and almost fell. Mama was the first to reach her son. Holding him around the waist, she half-carried him to the house. Blood dripped on the snow. "My face," Robert cried. Lawrence stood frozen on the spot. The air spun around him. Mama's orders snapped him back.

"Tell Papa to harness the dogs. We need to find a doctor to fix Robert's face. Then run and get Kokom. I'll try to stop the bleeding." She pushed Robert into the house. The door closed behind them.

Papa was chopping wood in the forest behind the house. He stopped when he saw Lawrence race toward him.

"Robert is bleeding! Sport bit him. Mama says to harness the dogs," Lawrence shouted. "I'm going to get Kokom." As Papa hurried off, Lawrence sped to his grandmother's place. In minutes he was at her door. Panting hard, he told her the news. Without a word, Kokom was on her way down the hill with Lawrence following behind.

When they reached the house they saw Robert lying on the toboggan wrapped in a wool blanket. His face was tightly covered with one of Mama's clean cloths.

Robert's eyes were closed and Lawrence thought he was sleeping.

Holding Robert around the waist, Mama half-carried him to the house.

Suddenly Robert moaned and opened his eyes, then closed them again. A shiver flashed through Lawrence, but he tried not to show he was afraid.

Papa finished harnessing the dogs as Mama spoke quietly to Kokom and Lawrence. "I don't want Robert to hear," she said. "Can you get your medicine ready, Bella, in case the doctor or nurse is not in town?"

As the toboggan pulled away, Lawrence and his sisters stood beside Kokom. "Go into the house," their grandmother ordered them. "Stay inside. I'll be back soon." She disappeared up the trail.

Once inside the children sat at the kitchen table to wait. "I wonder when they'll be back," Lawrence said.

Margaret was crying. "Sport didn't mean it," she sobbed. "Will Robert get better?"

"The doctor will fix him up," Lawrence said hopefully.

"If the doctor is in town." Elizabeth frowned.

Lawrence got up and looked out the window. 'It was Robert's fault,' he thought, then felt guilty. His brother had let him ride his sled. On the other hand, everyone knew it was dangerous to tease dogs when they were being fed. He didn't know what to feel anymore.

He was still standing at the window when Kokom came in carrying her knapsack.

Grandmother spoke firmly as she put water on the stove to boil. "It's not a good thing to tease the animals that help us. Dogs should be treated well, just like people. They work for us and we need them. I hope you all have learned from this." Her words made Lawrence feel better. His brother would learn from his mistake.

Time passed slowly as they waited for the toboggan to return. Margaret and Elizabeth went to bed but Lawrence could not sleep. He sat with his grandmother, straining to hear the sounds of the dog team.

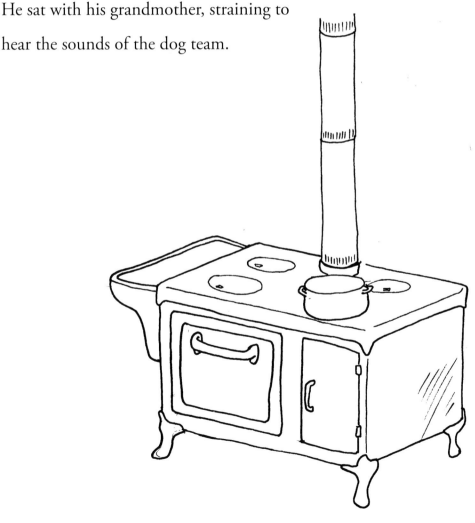

Chapter 9
Natural Medicine

As the toboggan pulled up outside the house, Lawrence and Kokom hurried to the door. Robert looked as if he was sleeping. Mama's face was grim, Papa was unsmiling.

"The district doctor and nurse were not around. I believe they were called away," Papa said, his lips tight. He lifted Robert off the toboggan and carried him into the house.

"Put Robert in bed," Kokom advised. While Robert slept, Papa went out to unharness the dogs.

Mama and Kokom sat at the table talking quietly about medicines. Lawrence stood nearby listening to them.

In the spring and summer, he walked with his mother to the sand ridges by the lake to pick medicine plants.

She taught him their names and how to use them. He didn't remember all of them, but he knew they were used for many ailments.

Kokom held up a piece of dried fungus. "This muskeg plant will stop the bleeding completely," she said. Lawrence followed his grandmother into the bedroom. Robert lay in bed, not speaking while she applied the spongy muskeg plant directly to his face.

Next she showed Mama and Lawrence some dried roots. "I'm boiling these for my grandson to drink. They will help to heal his wound from inside." When the tea was ready, she poured a cup and gave it to Lawrence.

"Take this to Robert," she said. Lawrence carefully carried the enamel tea cup to his brother's room as Kokom followed him in.

Mama sat on the edge of the bed watching Robert drink his tea. "Good. He finished it while it was hot. It works best that way," she informed Lawrence.

Feeling a little better, Robert struggled to get up.

"Don't even think about it. You have to stay in bed," Mama commanded him. Robert groaned and lay back down.

"Listen to your mother," Kokom added. Then she motioned to Lawrence. "We'll leave Robert to rest."

Lawrence glanced back at his brother's frowning face as they left the bedroom. What would his older brother do next? He knew Robert hated to stay still.

"You'll be fine if you get your rest," Mama said as she tucked in Robert's blanket. As she headed to the door, Robert spoke. "Do you have any old spools?" He asked weakly. "I want to carve spinning tops for Lawrence and the girls." Mama smiled. She soon brought back his pocketknife and three empty wooden spools that once held her sewing thread.

"Tops will make them happy," she approved, "and carving them will keep you out of trouble. After all that's happened, I'm sure you will never tease a dog again."

Robert looked pretty sure too.

New Year's Eve was only a few days away. As he ate his supper, Lawrence wondered if his older brother would come with them to the party in town, but he didn't have the courage to ask.

Chapter 10
The Moon
Speaks Cree

Lawrence's family rode the long toboggan to the New Year's Eve party. Even Robert was with them, carefully wrapped in a blanket to protect his face from the cold. Lawrence patted the spinning top his brother had carved for him. He kept it snugly in his shirt pocket.

As they neared the home of Papa's good friend, Lawrence saw that it was already filled with people. More were arriving from every direction. All the toboggans were bright with colourful yarns and merry with jingling bells.

Lawrence jumped off the toboggan and ran past the outside fire where pots of tea and coffee were kept steaming hot. He raced into the house.

In Cree, New Year's Day is called ocehtokisikaw, "kissing day." Inside the house, guests greeted each other loudly, then hugged and kissed. "Help yourself to food," the host called out. Some guests piled plates with moose ribs and potatoes.

Lawrence ate bannock and tasty smoked whitefish from the lake.

The sound of fiddlers drew him into the living room. Arms pumping, feet tapping, the fiddlers played one lively tune after another. Dancers swirled around, their feet a blur of steps.

Lawrence's mouth dropped. In the middle of the floor, Papa and Kokom Bella were high-stepping to the Red River Jig. He couldn't take his eyes off them. It was the first time he'd ever seen his grandma dance.

Papa's back was straight and his feet lifted high off the floor. Kokom's feet moved so fast Lawrence couldn't see what they were doing. "More! More!" Cheered the guests.

When the song ended, Papa and Kokom caught their breaths. "Your grandmother was a high-stepping young woman in her time," Papa told Lawrence. "I had to get her to dance before she forgot how to do it."

"I feel young again," Kokom beamed at Lawrence. She sat down to rest beside Mosoom Albert. To keep them company, Lawrence sat across from them with Mama.

Mosoom sat without moving for a long time. His eyes did not leave the fiddlers. Lawrence watched him closely. Mama leaned over. "Why are you staring at your grandfather?" She asked quietly so Mosoom would not hear.

In the middle of the floor, Papa and Kokom were high-stepping to the Red River Jig.

Lawrence wasn't sure what to say. "There are sparkles on his eyes," he finally said, "and sometimes he smiles to himself."

Mama put her arm around her son. "Those are tears that sparkle. The light from the gas lamp makes them shine."

"Are they sparkles like the diamonds Elizabeth talks about?"

Mama paused, and then spoke. "If memories can bring tears to one's eyes, they are worth more than diamonds. Mosoom is remembering happy times of long ago. I'm sure he has many memories. He was the best fiddle player in this part of the country."

"Mosoom plays the fiddle?" Lawrence exclaimed in surprise. "Why doesn't he ever play for us?"

"When he was young, your grandfather played the fiddle all the time."

"I love fiddle music," Lawrence said.

"That was the problem. Everyone loved his fiddle music. They stayed up all Saturday night dancing and jigging and they didn't go to church on Sunday. That's when Mosoom was told to stop playing the fiddle."

"I don't understand," Lawrence said. "Who told him?"

"The church people," Mama replied. "They blamed him because we didn't go to church. They said his music was possessed by the devil. Mosoom didn't want trouble so he simply stopped playing his fiddle. But he never stopped loving it."

She kissed Lawrence. "Go over and give your grandpa a hug and tell him you love him."

With a last thoughtful look at Mama, Lawrence did as he was told. The words came easily. "Thank you for everything you are teaching me," Lawrence said. "I love you." He hugged his grandfather tightly.

Mosoom's eyes shone this time with happiness. "Thank you, Grandson. You have made me feel good tonight." He hugged Lawrence again and then pointed to the window. "Now it's almost the New Year. Join the other children and watch the celebration. Then go and kiss everyone for me."

The men had gone outside carrying their rifles. A voice shouted, "It's the New Year." Rifles echoed as they shot into the air. Inside the house, women and children banged pots and pans. Voices called out, "Happy New Year!" Dogs barked and howled along with them.

Mosoom's eyes shone …

After the noise died down, all the guests gathered inside. The fiddlers played a gentle waltz. Husbands and wives, adults and children danced happily together.

Long after midnight, Lawrence and his family rode home on the toboggan pulled by the dogs. Overhead, a full moon hung in a star-filled sky. To Lawrence, it seemed to say, "Miyo nipa. Sleep well."

Lawrence murmured to himself, "Some day when I'm old, I'll remember tonight. Maybe I will have diamonds in my eyes."

As the toboggan swayed from side to side, he fell asleep.

Epilogue

The Moon Speaks Cree is based on the traditional Cree childhood of award-winning author Larry Loyie. In this entertaining story, the author authentically captures the closeness of traditional Aboriginal family life in the early 1940s.

Welcome to winter, a fascinating season in young Lawrence's life. As the snow begins to fall, Lawrence and his sisters Margaret and Elizabeth embrace the adventures that winter brings. They try to catch a snowflake, ride on their Papa's toboggan, and invent an amazing slider to whiz down the snow on Rabbit Hill.

The story also shares deeper lessons: respect for culture and history, the effect of change on Aboriginal people, and the importance of being good to animals.

Lawrence's father teaches him the secrets of winter survival and how to care for his long toboggan and the four special dogs that pull it. His mother creates a warm home environment as the family prepares for the celebrations of Christmas and New Year's Day. Mama teaches Lawrence to respect others, to share with his siblings, and to understand the changing role of his older brother Robert.

The younger children envy Robert's fancy sled with its steel runners and want to try it out on Rabbit Hill. With heavy hearts, they learn that their older brother needs it for school and work. Lawrence is inspired by his grandmother Kokom Bella's advice of "make do with what you have" and invents an amazing slider out of an old steamer trunk that once belonged to his grandfather who died in the flu epidemic of 1918. His invention works so well it even catches Robert's attention.

After Papa returns from his annual winter foray into the bush to make money to support his family, the joy of the Christmas feast is shared by all, including Kokom Bella. A visit from Mosoom Albert, Lawrence's gentle grandfather, makes the day complete.

When Robert teases one of the toboggan dogs, dire consequences result. Lawrence is confused about his feelings when Robert is injured. With Kokom's help, he comes to understand that there is an important lesson to be learned from the mishap.

While resting in bed, Robert carves spinning tops for Lawrence and his sisters. Tucked into Lawrence's shirt pocket, the top is a treasured gift, a reminder of the closeness of family.

On New Year's Eve, the family ride Papa's toboggan to a festive celebration. Ocehtokisikaw, "kissing day" in Cree, draws family and friends together to enjoy each other's company and eat tasty traditional foods such as moose stew and whitefish from the lake. Perhaps best of all, they jig to the music of the fast-fingered Cree and Métis fiddlers playing lively tunes such as the Red River Jig. To Lawrence's surprise and delight, even Kokom Bella displays her dancing skills.

At the party, Lawrence learns of his Mosoom Albert's secret sorrow. Mama explains that his grandfather was the best fiddle player around until he was told by church people that his music came from the devil. To avoid trouble, Albert stopped playing his fiddle. As Lawrence learns, his grandfather never stopped loving the music that so clearly reflects the joy of Aboriginal culture.

Talking Points for Classrooms

Author Larry Loyie (known as Lawrence as a child) lived a traditional Aboriginal life until he was nine years old and went to residential school. He loved this traditional life and wants to share it with today's readers. The book takes place in the early 1940s, a time of change for Aboriginal families. Although Lawrence and his family lived near a town, they still relied on nature to provide them with much of what they needed for survival.

In *The Moon Speaks Cree*, Larry Loyie describes a winter filled with adventures, family relationships, and learning about Aboriginal culture and way of life.

Ideas for Discussion:

1. What is a "traditional" Aboriginal lifestyle?
2. What survival traditions are in the book?
3. What family traditions are in the book?
4. What traditional knowledge is shared in the book?
5. Does your family have traditions? Do you have your own traditions?
6. What is the importance of dogs in Lawrence's family's life?

7. Name some ways that his family is good to their dogs.

8. Do you have a pet in your life? How do you feel about your pet? How do you care for your pet?

9. What are ways that Lawrence shows his love and respect for his grandmother (Kokom Bella) and grandfather (Mosoom Albert)?

10. What does Lawrence learn from Kokom Bella? She encouraged Lawrence to "make do with what you have." Does he take her advice? What does he invent?

11. Robert, Lawrence's older brother, is almost a man. His new responsibilities influence his relationship with his younger brother and sisters. What are the ways that Robert is now different from them? How does Robert show his positive feelings for them?

12. What have you learned from others in your family?

13. Mama tells Lawrence about Mosoom Daniel, his Papa's father who died in the flu epidemic of 1918. Research more about this worldwide flu epidemic.

14. Lawrence's grandfather, Mosoom Albert, gave up a special skill related to his culture. In your own words, explain what happened. Talk about why you think this happened. Would you make the same choice as Mosoom Albert?

15. Is the ending of *The Moon Speaks Cree* happy or sad? Explain why you feel this way.

16. How is your life today similar to Lawrence's life in the early 1940s? How is it different?

Talking points provided by Principal Christine Gullion of Oski Pasikoniwew Kamik, a K4-K7 school on Bigstone Cree Nation, Wabasca, Alberta, Canada. This Cree-based school practises cultural traditions along with its regular curriculum.

Glossary
With Pronunciation

1. Mosoom *(moo-sum)* – Grandfather

2. Kokom *(ko-cum)* – Grandmother

3. Tansi *(tan-sey)* – Hello

4. Kayas *(ka-yas)* – It's been a long time

5. Wihkasin *(whi-ka-sin)* – Tasty

6. Ocehtokisikaw *(o-chi-to-kisi-gow)* – Kissing Day,

   New Year's Day

7. Miyo nipa *(me-yo-ne-pa)* – Sleep well

Additional Artwork

Biographies

Larry Loyie is an award-winning Cree author, born in Slave Lake, Alberta. *The Moon Speaks Cree* is the fourth book in his "Lawrence Series." His first book *As Long as the Rivers Flow* (Groundwood) received the Norma Fleck Award for Canadian Children's Non-Fiction and was the 2006 First Nation Communities Read Honour Book. A residential school survivor, Larry Loyie's chapter book *Goodbye Buffalo Bay* (Theytus) is the evocative sequel to *As Long as the Rivers Flow*, the true story of his last year in residential school and of moving on. *When the Spirits Dance* (Theytus) is his family's story during the Second World War. *The Gathering Tree* (Theytus), winner of a Moonbeam Children's Book medal, is a best-selling fictional family story encouraging HIV awareness. The author takes care to ensure his books are truthful and accurate. Larry Loyie's website is **www.firstnationswriter.com**

Constance Brissenden (BA, MA) is a writer, editor and longtime collaborator with Larry Loyie.

Dr. Bill Cohen (Ed.D., M.Ed., BA & Sc.) is an Okanagan Nation artist and educator. He has taught for more than twenty-five years and is a language and community activist. He was mentored by Sqilxʷ Elders and leaders throughout his life.